Game of Hearts

Adapted by M. C. King

Based on the series created by Michael Poryes and Rich Correll & Barry O'Brien

Part One is based on the episode, "You Are So Sue-able to Me," Written by Sally Lapiduss

Part Two is based on the episode, "My Best Friend's Boyfriend," Written by Jay J. Demopoulos

DISNEP PRESS

New York

Printed in the United States of America

First Edition
1 3 5 7 9 10 8 6 4 2

Library of Congress Control Number: 2007909638
ISBN: 978-1-4231-0973-0

For more Disney Press fun, visit www.disneybooks.com
Visit DisneyChannel.com

PART ONE

Chapter One

Miley Stewart had seen her share of grossness in the school cafeteria, but this was extreme. She sat in baffled silence, her fork poised above her plate, watching two guys at the next table lob meatballs into each other's mouths. "He goes from the top of the key, he shoots, he scores!" Nick shouted. Todd caught the meatball in his gaping mouth, then grinned proudly. Tomato sauce dribbled down his chin. Ugh, thought Miley, feeling nauseous. Where were these guys raised? A barn?

"I can't believe Justin Timberlake is from the same species. Some boys are such pigs," she said with a frown, then turned toward her best friend, Lilly Truscott.

But Lilly hadn't heard her. She was totally focused on her lunch. Spaghetti strands dangled from Lilly's lips as she slowly slurped. Miley couldn't believe her eyes. Or her ears! Lilly was slurping with gusto—and volume! What was happening? Was it Be-as-Disgusting-as-You-Can-Be Day at school today? Had someone forgotten to send Miley the e-mail? "Lilly!" Miley raised her voice.

A distracted Lilly looked up from her plate. "Wha?" she grumbled, her mouth full of spaghetti.

"Close your mouth!" Miley exclaimed.

She couldn't help feeling a little embarrassed for Lilly. "We're in the ninth grade. You gotta start acting more like a, oh, I don't know . . . a girl?"

Lilly scowled, tugging at the ski cap she was wearing over her tangled, unbrushed hair. "What are you talking about? I act like a girl all the time."

"Incoming!" they heard Todd scream as a meatball flew toward them. Miley braced herself for the splat, while Lilly leaped to her feet and caught the meatball one-handed with expert precision. "Truscott from downtown!" she yelled, shooting it back into Todd's mouth. "Booyah!" she hooted triumphantly. She ran over to give the guys high fives.

Boo-yah. Miley hated when Lilly said "boo-yah." It was so *guylike*. And not supersuave-hottie-Justin Timberlake guylike, but gross-junior-high-school-food-fighting-video-game-playing guylike. Miley wasn't sure why watching Lilly pal around with the guys bugged her so much. But it did, it really did. And she wasn't alone.

Amber Addison and Ashley Dewitt were two of the meanest girls at school—and proud of it. They never missed an opportunity to make fun of someone. They spied Lilly messing around with the guys from across the cafeteria and promptly made a beeline for her. "Nice shot, Mr. Man," Amber told Lilly in a mocking tone.

"*Muy* macko," Ashley sniped. Ashley was what Miley's dad would call "not the brightest bulb."

"It's *macho*," Amber corrected her.

"Whatever," Ashley said, rolling her eyes. "You know I'm bad at French."

Lilly looked at the girls in annoyance.

Like she cared what Amber and Ashley thought!

"Well, at least I know how to be a girl!" Ashley snapped. Then she and Amber sauntered off, laughing.

Lilly scuffed back to the table, looking irritated. Usually, Miley would have said something against Ashley and Amber, like how obvious it was that they were just jealous of Lilly and the attention Todd and Nick gave her. But today, Miley saw their point. "I never thought this day would come," she said, shaking her head at Lilly forlornly, "but . . . Amber and Ashley are right."

Lilly looked flabbergasted. "They are *not* right," she argued. Miley noticed a spaghetti stain on the front of Lilly's hoodie. When Lilly caught Miley staring at the stain, her face turned bright red. "I know how to be a girl," she exclaimed defensively.

"Then how come you don't have a date for the dance Friday night?" Miley asked.

"Not everybody's going to the dance," Lilly huffed. "*You're* not going."

Miley lowered her voice. "I've got a Hannah concert," she whispered. Miley had a secret that only a few people knew. She wasn't just a regular ninth grader. She was also Hannah Montana, chart-topping pop sensation. But a downside was that her weekends were often booked.

"Details, details," said Lilly, turning glum. Being best friends with Miley wasn't always the easiest. Here she was, feeling bad because she didn't have a date for a dumb high school dance, while Miley didn't even have to think about it. It wasn't fair.

Miley saw the crestfallen look on Lilly's

face. "I'm not going to let you give up," she said encouragingly. "There's a ninth-grade girl in there, and I'm going to get her out." Miley was excited to have a project—one that didn't involve school or singing. Plus, Lilly deserved to be happy. And knowing she could help make Lilly happy made Miley happy!

Now, where to start? Miley looked Lilly up and down. Well, she thought, might as well start at the top. She yanked off Lilly's woolen hat so that her long hair came tumbling out. Yikes, bed head. Ooooh, and split ends. Still, it was an improvement. Next up: Lilly's horrific posture. "Quit sitting like a guy," Miley said, pushing Lilly's back upright.

"Like that is gonna do any good," Lilly grumbled.

"Well," Miley said, a smile spreading

across her face as she gazed across the cafeteria, "it looks like it's working for Matt Marshall." There was Matt Marshall, the totally sweet skateboarder who Lilly had had a crush on forever. And he was coming toward them!

"Hey, Lilly," Matt said. He was wearing a green T-shirt over a white thermal top and board shorts. Kinda like what Lilly wears every day, Miley thought to herself.

"'Sup, Matt?" Lilly said, going immediately into one-of-the-guys mode. She raised her fist to bump his.

"Act like a girl," Miley reminded Lilly through gritted teeth.

Apparently, the girl thing didn't come naturally to Lilly. "So, Matthew . . ." She paused awkwardly, not knowing what to say next. "Come here often?"

Now Lilly sounded like some cornball

breath-mint commercial! "Of course he does," Miley said, coughing, "it's school!"

Thankfully, Matt wasn't derailed. "So, are you going to this dance on Friday?" he asked Lilly. "I just thought if you were going, we could maybe . . ."

"Carpool?" Lilly interrupted him.

"No, I kinda meant . . ." Matt was looking nervous himself now.

"Yeah?" Lilly waited for him to say something else.

"What?" Matt asked in confusion.

"What?" said Lilly.

Miley had heard enough. "Oh, sweet niblets! Of course she'll go to the dance with you!"

"Cool!" said Matt.

"Cool!" said Lilly.

How do I do it? Miley wondered.

Chapter Two

Later that day after school, Miley found Lilly at Rico's Surf Shop. She was standing at the bar in a huddle of guys watching *Teen Court*.

"Lilly," Miley said, pulling her from the crowd, "I hope you've got your shopping shoes on 'cause I'm going to take you from skate chick to *date* chick."

"One second," Lilly said, pointing to the TV. "It's almost over."

These days, *Teen Court* was just about everybody's favorite show. Who wouldn't like watching a judge "serve" high schoolers justice by pouring buckets of stinky food onto their heads? Still, it wasn't Miley's favorite thing to do after school—especially when there were more exciting things. Like shopping.

"Serve it up! Serve it up!" Lilly and the guys screamed. Miley glanced at the TV screen hanging above the bar. Judge Joe had given his verdict, and now the guilty teen was being doused with a vat of cold, maple-syrupy oatmeal. Yuck.

"Dude, he got served!" Lilly roared, high-fiving the guys. "Breakfast, lunch, and—" She turned to discover Miley staring knowingly at her. Lilly's face fell. Busted for acting like a guy again. "This is what you were talking about, right?" she asked.

"Yeah," Miley answered, pulling Lilly out of earshot.

"Look, just because Matt already asked you to the dance doesn't mean he can't change his mind. You know, you got him nibblin' on the cheese, but now you gotta snap the trap!" Miley had enough experience to know—not only were guys sometimes immature, they also were often fickle.

"Miley, he already asked me," Lilly said. "It's not like he's going to dump me and ask some—" She stopped midsentence, her eyes growing wide. Just as she'd been prattling on about how Matt would never ditch her, she spied him hanging out with . . . Ashley and Amber! "What is he doing?" she shrieked.

"Looks like someone's messin' with your man," Miley said, shaking her head.

Lilly watched Ashley and Amber with

disbelief. They'd never noticed Matt before. But now that he was going on a date with her, they were all over him. "That's it," Lilly said, gripped with sudden determination. "I'm through being one of the guys." She turned to Miley. She was at her mercy. "Girl me up, baby."

Sweeter words Miley had never heard!

Chapter Three

Miley's older brother, Jackson, stood over the table, staring eagerly at the twenty-something cell phones before him. It was almost time.

"J-B-A-D, one-oh-nine-point-six, Los Angeles," the radio announced. "Now, get those dialing digits ready, 'cause the lucky twenty-fourth caller gets two courtside seats for this Sunday's play-off game featuring your Los Angeles Lllaaaakers!"

Jackson shook his hands out as if he himself were preparing for a game-winning foul shot. His dialing digits were as ready as they'd ever be when the announcer gave the countdown. "Three, two, one, go!" And with lightning speed, Jackson hit SEND on every phone.

Just then, Jackson looked up and spotted Thor, the new kid in the neighborhood, standing on the Stewarts' deck. He didn't know much about him, except that he had very bad timing! A friendly faced teddy bear of a guy, Thor loped his way over toward Jackson. Either he didn't notice that Jackson was busy, or he didn't care. "Hey, new buddy, how's it going?"

"Not now, Thor!" Jackson bristled. He didn't have anything personal against the guy, but couldn't Thor see he was busy?

Jackson picked up the phones, one by one, listening for a voice on the other end. Phone number one: busy signal . . . Phone number two: no answer . . . Phone number three: busy signal.

Not ten seconds later, Thor asked "How 'bout now?"

Jackson didn't want to be rude . . . but he had no choice. "No!" he snapped. "I'm trying to win a contest here, so just—"

Suddenly, a voice came from one of the phones. "Congratulations!" It was the radio announcer. "You're the lucky twenty-fourth caller!"

Jackson was stoked. "I did it! I won!" he shouted. Now if only he could find the phone that had gotten through . . . It sounded like the flip phone. Jackson picked it up. "Hello? Hello?" Busy signal. Maybe it was the silver one. Nope, static.

He could hear the radio announcer's voice. "If you're gone," the guy warned, "I'm moving on."

Jackson was frantic! Which phone? WHICH PHONE? Thor decided to pitch in. "Hello," he said, picking up a phone. A voice said something. "Oh, sorry," Thor apologized, "can't talk now." He tossed the phone off the deck. Jackson looked at him, mystified. "Holy cow," said Thor, realizing what he'd just done.

"You!" Jackson dove off the rail in a frenzy, screaming to the phone: "Don't hang up!"

Moments later, Jackson walked into the house, a triumphant smile on his face. He'd skinned his knee and scraped his arm, and there was a branch tangled in his hair, but he'd gotten to the announcer in time.

"Yes, thank you, thank you," he gushed. He couldn't stop grinning. "J-Bad rocks!" He hung up. In all the excitement, he'd almost forgotten that Thor was beside him.

"Wow," said Thor, impressed. "Courtside seats for the Lakers. You know what I'd do if I had courtside seats for the Lakers? I'd take you. 'Cause you're my new buddy. So, who are you gonna take?"

"Well, actually, Thor, I hadn't really thought—" Jackson was still flushed with the excitement of winning the contest. Thor was catching him off guard.

"Oh, I get it. You got lots of friends. I know what that's like. Back on the farm, I had lots of friends . . . and cows. . . . Okay, all my friends were cows . . . but they were good listeners . . . with their big brown eyes and sweet smiles."

Cows that were friends? Ack! Thor was

really laying it on thick. And he was hitting Jackson where it hurt. After all, Jackson knew what it was like to be new. To be from someplace far away and totally different. After all, you could still hear a trace of Tennessee twang in his voice. Jackson knew what it meant to be an outsider — lonely. He caved. "Thor, do you wanna go to the game?"

"Yes! Yes!" Happiness surged through Thor as he lifted Jackson off the ground. "Thank you, Jackson! You are the ice beneath my skates."

The ice beneath my skates? What had Jackson gotten himself into? "Don't ever say that again," Jackson said, ushering Thor to the door.

"Okeydokey, artichokey," Thor agreed.

"That either!" Jackson let out a big sigh. What had he done?

And it was about to get worse. No sooner had Thor left, than Jackson's father appeared. Mr. Stewart threw open the door, his face flushed with excitement, and bounded over to Jackson. "There he is!" he roared. "I just heard you on J-Bad! Eee, doggies! Me and my boy are gonna sit courtside at a play-off game! Can you believe this is happening?!"

Uh-oh . . .

Chapter Four

Lilly stood nervously in the hallway at school the next day, refusing to go into the classroom. Miley tried not to get angry. But it was really hard. Lilly was being so difficult and stubborn! Ugh! Miley thought. Did she have to remind Lilly that she'd gotten up at the crack of dawn to trek over to her house two hours before school started to give her a makeover? Not to mention the hours they'd spent yesterday at the mall. Miley had watched Lilly try on outfit after outfit, and had gone back and forth from the changing room to the racks to get different sizes and different colors. All this work, and now Lilly didn't even want to show her face?

"C'mon," Miley coaxed. It was difficult to hide her impatience. "Nobody's gonna laugh. You look great."

"I do not," Lilly whined. "I look like Amber and Ashley threw up on me. I can't do this."

Lilly might not want to show anyone how supercute she looked, but Miley felt her work deserved to be seen. For once, she'd been able to take advantage of being Hannah Montana. After all, she knew tons of stylists and makeup artists, and she'd managed to pick up a few pointers. It might have been hard work, but Miley had a blast honing her styling skills. She'd loved putting together Lilly's outfit: a hot pink sleeveless shirt over a dark denim skirt. And she'd loaded Lilly up with the cutest accessories: enormous shades, gold necklaces, giant hoop earrings, and sparkly bangles. She'd done Lilly's makeup using natural tones with just a hint of pink. She'd even given her a manicure! And not only a manicure—a French manicure!

Miley had had it. It was now or never. Class started momentarily. She gave Lilly's arm one final tug, pulling her into the classroom. Poor Lilly came stumbling in—she wasn't used to walking in shoes that weren't sneakers or flip-flops.

Nick, the meatball lobber from the day before, was the first boy to notice the girl in the pink top. "Hey, new girl," he hooted. "Where'd you come from? Hotsylvania?"

Lilly had been blushing when she

walked in. But now her cheeks were practically the color of her shirt. "Shut up, Nick," she growled. "It's me."

"Whoa!" Nick's fellow meatballer, Todd, looked stunned. "The new girl sounds kinda like Lilly." Lilly knew she was supposed to act girly, but she couldn't stop herself. She punched Nick's arm.

"Ow!" Nick winced. He'd recognize that left hook anywhere. "It *is* Lilly!"

Lilly removed her gigantic sunglasses. The boys gasped in astonishment. "Lilly, what happened to you?" Todd asked. "You look *fine!*"

Fine? "Really?" Lilly couldn't believe it. They were talking about *her!*

"Totally," the guys said.

Miley just stood back and watched. Lilly was finally enjoying her makeover. Wait until Matt sees her, Miley thought happily.

Chapter Five

Jackson took a deep breath. Since the previous night, he'd been thinking about how he was going to handle the Lakers-game dilemma. He had to somehow tell Thor that he was going to take his dad to the game. He'd decided quick and painless was the best way to go.

He found Thor standing at his locker with his back to him. Great, Jackson thought. Maybe I should've just called him instead.

Jackson cleared his throat nervously. "Listen, Thor," he began. No beating around the bush, he coached himself. "About the play-off game—"

Thor whipped around to face Jackson. He was holding a giant cake in the shape of a basketball. "HAPPY, HAPPY PLAY-OFFS," Thor started singing. "MAY ALL YOUR DREAMS COME TRUE. I HOPE YOU LIKE THIS CARROT CAKE, MY MOM MADE IT FOR YOU!"

Jackson looked at Thor in disbelief. He had been expecting disappointment, resistance, maybe even tears. But a cake?

"It's a basketball cake," Thor announced proudly, even though it was pretty obvious. "And there's thirteen pounds of Minnesota cream cheese in there."

"Yeah, it looks great," Jackson muttered.

"It should," said Thor. "Mom stayed up

all night baking it. She's so happy I finally have a friend. Anyhoo, what were you gonna say about the game?"

Quick and painless, quick and painless, quick and painless. Jackson prepared himself to break the news to Thor. He had to take his dad to the game. It was a family obligation.

But then he caught the desperate look in Thor's eyes. And the cake did smell good. Thor's mom seemed like an awfully nice woman. Jackson wouldn't want to disappoint her. "You're paying for parking!" he sputtered.

Shoot! He'd wimped out. Jackson ran up the stairs and headed to class, giant cake in hand, wondering what he was going to do. He passed a crowd of freshmen talking to a girl who looked familiar . . . except . . . different.

Could it be?

Was that . . .

Lilly?

Miley hadn't just coached Lilly on her appearance. They'd worked on her behavior, too—*especially* where boys were concerned. Lilly was always acting like one of the guys. She played sports with them, talked video games with them, got into burping contests with them. According to Miley, if Lilly wanted to keep Matt, she'd have to stop doing all of these things—especially the last one. *Burping*? Gross!

Also? She'd have to play up to them. Miley had never met a guy who didn't like a little ego-stroking. "Oh, Todd, you're so funny," Lilly cooed—at least, she tried to coo. Miley said she still had a lot of work to do on that.

"So, 'new Lilly,' want to hang at the

dance with me?" Todd asked.

Miley didn't want Lilly to have to disappoint anyone. As a good friend, she took it upon herself to do it. "Sorry, boys," she told Lilly's admirers. "She's taken." She whisked Lilly off. Miley's pride was swelling. All her hard work sure was paying off! "I'm not just good," Miley congratulated herself. "I'm scary good."

Now, it was time for the real test: Matt! He was walking right toward them. He looked at Lilly in confusion.

"Lilly?" he asked hesitantly. Was that really her under all the makeup?

"Wow, you look so . . ." Matt was so stunned, he became speechless! It was the perfect moment for Lilly to say something charming. And Miley knew exactly what it should be! "And it's all for you," she whispered in Lilly's ear.

"And it's all for you," Lilly repeated. She gave him a big smile.

"I . . . I . . ." Matt stammered.

While poor Matt grew even more dumbfounded, Lilly became more and more confident. "Shhhh . . ." she said, lifting her finger to touch Matt's mouth. "Save it for the dance." It was a line straight out of a soap opera! Miley looked at her friend and gave her an approving glance.

The bell rang. Matt looked relieved. "Uh, bye," he said awkwardly, then scurried off.

"Save it for the dance?" Miley whooped excitedly. "Way to snap the trap!" She raised her hand expectantly.

But Lilly denied Miley the high five. "Nails," she explained, wiggling her newly polished fingertips in the air.

Miley had never felt so proud!

Chapter Six

That Friday night, Miley may have been onstage singing for a sold-out crowd as Hannah Montana, but . . . her mind was on Lilly and the dance. Lilly had promised to get in touch as soon as she and Matt got there. But between songs, Miley had checked to see if she'd gotten any texts — and *nothing*. She called Lilly during intermission and then again when the show was over. She got her voice mail both times.

No news is good news, somebody once said. Miley figured the reason she hadn't heard from Lilly was because the date was going really well.

So she was more than a little shocked when she arrived home and found Lilly curled in a ball on the deck chair. She was wearing the gorgeous dress Miley had helped her pick out that afternoon at the mall. It was green and shimmery, and it made Lilly's eyes sparkle. Except now they were glazed with tears.

"Lilly, what are you doing here?" Miley asked.

"He stood me up," Lilly said sadly.

Miley heard Lilly's words, but she had trouble processing them. "What?" Miley crouched next to the chair, so she and Lilly were eye to eye.

"I sat at home waiting for two hours,"

she replied quietly. She sniffled.

Suddenly, they heard footsteps on the deck. It was Mr. Stewart. "Lilly. Look at you," he beamed. "I betcha some hearts were broken tonight."

Lilly burst into tears. "Just one!" she cried.

"Way to go, Dad," Miley said.

The next day, Miley woke up early. For once, she didn't start the morning berating her dad about getting an orange juicer that had been made in this century. Using the old-timey one was good for releasing her frustration. Because not only were boys immature and fickle sometimes, they could also be downright mean!

"How can boys be so cruel?!" she asked her dad, twisting the orange half with brute force. She was going to squeeze every last drop of juice out of that thing if it killed her! "How could someone do something like that to Lilly? Don't they know how fragile and delicate we girls are?!"

Mr. Stewart grabbed the decimated orange from his daughter's hand and grimaced. His daughter? Delicate? "Sugar and spice and hands like a vice. Heaven help the boy who stands you up."

"You got that right, bub!"

"Morning," croaked Lilly as she entered the kitchen. She was wearing a pair of Miley's most comfy pajamas, though it didn't look like they'd helped her sleep.

"How are you feeling?" Miley asked.

"Okay," murmured Lilly, though from the look of Lilly's bloodshot eyes, she was anything but. Miley had heard Lilly tossing and turning all night.

Miley asked her dad if they could be

alone, then followed Lilly to the couch.

"Lilly, I just hate seeing you like this," Miley said. "It's not right. There's got to be a way to get him back for the pain and suffering he put you through."

"I'd like to know how," said Lilly. She let out a huge sigh.

Lilly reached for the remote. The TV turned on, and they were immediately confronted with Judge Joe's angry snarl. The booming voice of the *Teen Court* announcer filled the living room. "Have you been put through pain and suffering? Did someone do you wrong?"

"They did *her* wrong!" Miley responded, pointing to Lilly.

"Heck yeah!" Lilly agreed.

"Well, don't just sit there and take it," the announcer continued. "Take it to court — *Teen Court* — where justice is served!"

Miley looked at Lilly.

Lilly looked at Miley.

They looked back at the TV.

Then back at each other.

Was Miley thinking what Lilly thought she was thinking?

Was Lilly thinking what Miley thought she was thinking?

Chapter Seven

Jackson was determined that the conversation with his dad go better than the one with Thor. This time, he'd hold strong. He wouldn't wimp out. Quick and painless—that was his motto.

He entered the house, the tickets in his hand. They'd arrived by Priority Mail that afternoon, and just looking at them gave Jackson's spine an electrifying chill.

Never had a word looked so promising, so beautiful, to Jackson, as COURTSIDE. All his life he'd dreamed of sitting courtside.

Mr. Stewart was on the phone. "Oh, who *cares* if your boy got into Harvard," Jackson overheard him say. "My boy's taking me to the Lakers game."

Oh, man! Jackson thought to himself. Mr. Stewart turned and smiled at Jackson, motioning that he'd just be another minute. "Courtside seats," he boasted to his buddy on the phone. "He could've taken anybody he wanted to, but he's taking the old man. Okay, I gotta run. I gotta give my boy a big bear hug. Talk at'cha later."

A bear hug! Jackson was a sucker for a bear hug! He could feel his determination melt away.

Mr. Stewart put down the phone and

turned to Jackson, his arms wide. "My boy!" Mr. Stewart beamed.

And poor Jackson wimped out again.

What was he going to do? The tickets were for tonight! Thor would be there in a matter of hours.

Jackson had to do something drastic. Something that didn't involve talking. Something that involved . . . action! He took a trip to the joke store, followed by a quick stop at Rico's, because Jackson's new plan required props.

With a little more than an hour until the game, Jackson got the plan underway. He grabbed a half-eaten burrito from a greasy bag, took a giant chomp, then called for Mr. Stewart.

"What's up, good buddy?" Mr. Stewart asked.

With his mouth full, Jackson said, "I just

wanted to tell you how much I'm looking forward to being at that game with you tonight, side by side, right next to each other." He shifted in his seat.

Pffffft!

Perfect! The whoopee cushions Jackson had purchased were doing their job. From the horrified look on his dad's face, it had all been worth it.

"Excuse me," Jackson said with a grimace. He pointed to his stomach, wincing in pretend pain. "You know what these burritos do to me."

Pffffft!

Jackson clutched his side.

"Are you gonna be all right for the game tonight, son?" Mr. Stewart asked looking concerned.

"Oh, I'm fine," said Jackson dismissively. "I just hope you don't mind, 'cause this is my third." He held up the burrito. "And I probably shouldn't have gone *con queso*." He made a subtle yet deliberate move to the right.

Pffffft!

It was a really loud one. Now Mr. Stewart didn't only look concerned, he also looked grossed out. He loved the Lakers, and he loved spending time with his son, but he had his limits. "You know, come to think of it . . ." he said. "I do have some paperwork to do. Maybe you could find somebody else to go with you."

It had worked! What a relief! Still, Jackson couldn't help playing it up a little bit more. This was actually kind of fun. "But, Dad," he whined, "it's supposed to be just the two of us."

Pffffft!
Pffffft!

Pfffffft!

"But if you really don't want to go, I could probably find somebody. . . ."

Just then, Thor arrived. As always, his timing was . . . bad. "Whoo!" he hollered. "Lakers rule! What time are we leaving?"

Jackson's eyes grew wide. Just when his plan was succeeding!

"Hey, maybe Thor would like to go," he said, trying to save face.

But it was too late. Thor had blown it. "Jackson?" Mr. Stewart said.

"What?" Jackson desperately tried to cover. "It's like fate," he insisted. "Him showing up as if I had invited him—which of course I hadn't!"

Mr. Stewart didn't say anything. He just stood there waiting for an explanation. "All right, fine," Jackson relented. "I invited Thor first, but then you went all 'my boy' on me, and he gave me that 'basketball death cake'—I gained five pounds just lookin' at the thing! I screwed up. I'm sorry. I'm a terrible person. I don't deserve to go. Why don't you guys just take the tickets." Defeated, he held out the tickets— the once-in-a-lifetime COURTSIDE tickets.

But nobody reached for them. "No, son," said Mr. Stewart. Jackson slumped, waiting for his dad to dig into him. Except his dad didn't sound angry—not even a little bit. "I screwed up," Mr. Stewart admitted, "and *I'm* sorry."

Huh? Jackson thought.

"They were your tickets, and I just invited myself along. You were just trying not to hurt the old man's feelings. And that means more to me than any old silly basketball game." Mr. Stewart grabbed Jackson in a hug, and Jackson was so caught in the moment he forgot that Thor was still there. That is, until Thor had made himself comfortable on the couch.

Pfffffft!

"Okay," a red-faced Thor tried to explain. "I know what you're thinking. But that was not me."

Chapter Eight

In person, the theme song to *Teen Court* sounded even more sinister. Not that Miley was nervous. As she and Lilly stood in the hall, waiting for their cue to enter the courtroom, Miley felt as confident as ever. Justice was going to be served. In the name of cruel, insensitive boys everywhere, Matt was going down! All she and Lilly had to do was present their case, then shoot down whatever lame-o defense he managed to come up with. "Easy-peasy," as Miley's Uncle Earl used to say.

"Thirty seconds," the assistant director warned them. Miley smoothed down the front of her suit and made sure her glasses weren't crooked on her nose. She was proud of the professional ensemble she'd created. She looked just like a lawyer on one of those courtroom shows her dad watched every night. She'd even slicked back her hair, then tied it up in an oh-so-serious bun.

Lilly fidgeted next to her. Miley was equally proud of the look she'd fashioned for Lilly: a pale yellow suit over a frilly pink top. She wore a prim headband in her hair and had on a pair of dainty white gloves. Lilly complained that they made her hands itch, but Miley forced her to keep them on. They made Lilly look ladylike, and everyone knew ladylike meant innocent.

A production assistant called for silence on the set. "Welcome to *Teen Court*," the announcer bellowed. "Today we hear the case of 'Diss'd, Dumped, and Dateless.' First, let's meet our defendant, Matt Marshall, high school sophomore and alleged dumper."

Matt stormed past Miley and Lilly. It was odd to see him so furious, when at school he was always superchill. Miley knew it had all been an act! The doors to the courtroom opened, and Matt stalked in. Lilly gulped. They were next. "And now our dumpee is entering the courtroom," the announcer said.

Miley escorted a shaky Lilly up the aisle. She saw Matt slumped over his podium and couldn't help herself. "You're going down, pal!" she snarled. "You're going down!"

"All rise for the honorable Judge Joe Barrett," the bailiff instructed.

Judge Joe was smaller than he looked on TV. Still, as he sat down in the judge's chair, he cast an imposing shadow over the courtroom. Lilly gulped again. The audience grew silent.

"When I first read this case," Judge Joe told the courtroom. "I pushed it to the top of my docket. You want to know why?" He turned to Matt and gave him a menacing stare. "Because I have a daughter, hotshot."

Matt humbly hung his head.

"Oh, *yeah*," Judge Joe growled.

This was going to be easier than Miley thought. The judge was already on their side! "Slam dunk, baby," she whispered to Lilly.

Judge Joe turned his attention to Lilly. His tone was gentle. "Now, sweetheart, it says here that you're suing for the cost of dress, hair, and makeup. Is that true, darling?" Lilly gripped a delicate handkerchief and let out a pained whimper. "Don't forget the shoes," she said with a shudder.

Miley nudged her. Time to turn it up a notch. "Tears," she whispered.

Lilly's shudder became a throaty sob. "And a mani-pedi," she bawled.

Judge Joe shook his head disapprovingly at Matt. "This girl got a mani-pedi for you?"

"I can explain," Matt said. He squirmed uncomfortably. He'd exchanged his usual T-shirt and board shorts for a dress shirt and tie. He looked as awkward as he felt.

"You'll have your chance," Judge Joe snapped. He turned back to Lilly. "Now tell me what happened, angel."

Despite Judge Joe's soothing tone, Lilly

quivered. "My friend is too upset to speak," Miley said, jumping in. "So she's asked me to plead her case."

Lilly waved her handkerchief in the distraught way that she and Miley had practiced at home. Judge Joe seemed to understand. "Go on and proceed, baby girl," he told Miley.

Miley had the fire in her belly—that was something else her Uncle Earl used to say. It meant that she felt angry and fierce and couldn't hold back. She strode to the front of the courtroom. "Your honor, ladies and gentlemen of the jury, what would this country be if men didn't keep their promises? What if George Washington promised to cross the Delaware but didn't because it was too chilly outside!"

The audience gasped audibly. Ooh, that had worked. So Miley broke out another one. "What if Abraham Lincoln promised to save the union but broke that promise because he wanted to buy a new hat?"

They nodded appreciatively. Miley was on a roll! She couldn't seem to stop! "What if Rutherford B. Hayes—"

The pounding of the gavel interrupted her. Judge Joe motioned for her to approach the bench. Wow, had he already reached a decision? She knew she was compelling, but she didn't realize she was *that* compelling! If the Hannah Montana gig didn't work out, maybe there was law school in Miley's future. Even if the Hannah Montana gig *did* work out, maybe there was law school in her future. She'd be the first attorney/pop superstar. Beat that, Christina Aguilera!

She reached the judge's podium. "I know what you're thinking," Miley told Judge

Joe. "How does she do it without any notes?"

"I'll tell you what I'm thinking," Judge Joe corrected her. "If somebody doesn't get food dumped on them in the next five minutes, my audience is going to dump me." He reached down for a framed photo of a boat. "And if Joe gets dumped, Joe can't pay for his big boat. And Joe likes his big boat."

Oh. Miley promised to wrap it up quickly. She made a beeline for Matt. She got as close to him as she could, then sneered. "Okay, so you asked her out, you stood her up, and you broke her heart, and now all we want to know is why!" She raised her voice. "WHYYYYYY?"

On that note, Miley concluded her argument. With a satisfied nod, she returned to Lilly's side.

Chapter Nine

"**Y**our honor," Matt began.

As interested as Miley was to hear whatever drivel Matt had come up with, she couldn't help heckling him. "Come on, come on—he hasn't got all day!" she snapped.

"This isn't fair!" Matt protested. "I only changed my mind." He motioned to Lilly. "She changed her . . . everything." Miley could feel Lilly quiver next to her. Matt continued. "I asked out a really cool skater girl, and the next day she was all girly and frilly and . . . weird. She just wasn't the girl I had a crush on."

Now that was just downright unfair, thought Miley. Just because Lilly looked like an actual ninth-grade girl for once, Matt had the nerve to punish her for it. Not only could guys be immature, fickle, and mean sometimes, they also could be really unfair!

She nudged Lilly as if to say "Get a load of this guy!" Except she couldn't get Lilly's attention. Lilly was focused entirely on Matt.

"You had a crush on me?" Lilly asked.

"Yeah," Matt admitted.

They stared intensely at each other. Forget the cameras and the judge and the audience—it was as if they were the only two people in the courtroom.

"Is this true?" Judge Joe asked Lilly. "Did you change?"

"Well," Lilly said, taking a moment to think, "she made me." She pointed to Miley.

What?! Miley was horrified that Lilly could say something so shocking, so unbelievable, so . . . true.

Suddenly, all eyes in the courtroom were on Miley—and not in a good way. Everyone was looking at her as if she'd done something wrong, when all she had tried to do was help—to be a good friend. No, a great friend! "I was just trying to turn her into a ninth grader," Miley told the judge. "I mean, you should've seen the way she looked before."

The audience gasped.

"I liked the way she looked before." Matt

sounded offended on Lilly's behalf.

"You did?" Lilly gazed gratefully across the courtroom.

Miley fumed. Lilly couldn't give up now! This guy stood her up! Revenge was almost theirs! "Oh, what does he know?" She scoffed. "Has he ever read a teen fashion magazine? I think not. He doesn't know what he wants. He needs to be told what he wants. He's a boy!" Miley was so consumed with the unfairness of it all, she didn't even notice when Lilly left her side and joined Matt at the other podium.

Miley was all alone. She glanced over at Lilly and Matt. They did look sweet together, although it would probably look more natural if Lilly were wearing her regular clothes. Seeing how happy Lilly looked, it finally dawned on Miley to ask herself why she had insisted Lilly "act like a girl?" Girls could be anything they wanted to be. So when Lilly was being Lilly—burping, high-fiving, screaming "boo-yah" —she *was* acting like a girl. Being a girl meant you can act whatever way you wanted, Miley thought.

Miley sighed. She realized she had some soul-searching to do. Not to mention, some apologizing, first to Lilly and then to Matt. Because after everything, it turned out that evil Matt wasn't evil at all. He wasn't immature or fickle. He wasn't downright mean or unfair. Okay, yeah, he should have called to cancel the date with Lilly instead of standing her up. But if Lilly could forgive him for that, Miley could, too—she guessed.

She was deep in thought when Judge Joe said: "Well, I'll tell you what I want. I want to serve up some justice. And I think

I know just who I want to serve it up to."

"Serve it up, serve it up," the audience chanted. Miley turned helplessly from the audience to Judge Joe as she realized what was about to happen. She made a panicked dash over to Lilly and Matt. "Isn't the important thing that these two wonderful kids are back together?" she asked the judge. "Isn't that why we're all here?"

But Judge Joe wasn't listening. Production assistants began handing out protective plastic ponchos to the audience.

"Okay, I admit it!" Miley said, throwing her hands up in the air. "Lilly, I'm sorry. I never should've tried to change you. You're great the way you are. Forgive me?"

"Sure, whatever," Lilly said dreamily. If she was mad at Miley, she was going to tell her about it later. Right now, she could only think about one thing—Matt!

"How about that?" Miley clamored, trying not to sound as desperate as she felt. "Everybody's happy. Another *Teen Court* case is closed. I think our work here is done!" She turned on her heels to exit the courtroom.

At that moment, Judge Joe pounded his gavel. The courtroom darkened. And the blinding hot spotlight hit Miley. "Oh, boy," was all she could say before the industrial-sized cans of spaghetti dripping in tomato sauce came cascading down from the ceiling.

Miley caught a glob of sauce in her mouth. Boo-yah, she thought, licking her lips. Actually, it didn't taste that bad.

The announcer gave the play-by-play. "Today's guilty party gets a heaping plate of spaghetti smothered in a hearty tomato sauce! And topped with plenty of squirmy, oily anchovies!"

Ewwwww! Anchovies! Slimy and stinky

and everywhere! Down her shirt and in her hair. She could feel one slither down her pant leg and into her sock. Miley fished one out of her right ear.

Judge Joe banged his gavel one last time. Case closed.

"Where'd you get these anchovies, Joe?" Miley called out. "Fishin' on your big boat?!"

With a swish of his long black robe, the judge left the courtroom without looking back. Soon, the audience was gone. Lilly and Matt, too. Miley shook herself out like a wet dog, sending splatters of tomato sauce everywhere. It was going to take a lot of baths to get the stench out. But Miley would use the time to think about everything she'd done—and why sometimes girls could be so *immature*.

PART TWO

Chapter One

Miley Stewart had learned a lot so far in the ninth grade: quadrilaterals, past participles, how to say "Where's the bathroom?" in Spanish. But of everything she'd learned, the most important lesson had been this: when it comes to boyfriends and best friends, life gets *really* complicated.

So, while she was thrilled to see Lilly having an awesome time with her latest crush, she couldn't help feeling a little nervous. Because it seemed like whenever one of them got together with a guy, something bad happened. First there had been the infamous Jake-asks-Lilly-to-the-school-dance-even-though-he-actually-likes-Miley fiasco. Then there had been the more recent Matt-likes-Lilly-until-Miley-messes-everything-up disaster.

Matt and Lilly hadn't turned out to be the romance Lilly had hoped it would be. But she'd recovered quickly and found a new guy that she was starting to like. His name was Lucas. He had shiny, light brown hair and a sweet smile. These days, Lilly and Lucas did everything together. They walked to class together, had lunch together, surfed together, watched TV together.

Now they were eating at an outdoor table at Rico's Surf Shop together. So far, they were just friends. But Miley could tell the relationship was headed for more. She couldn't help noticing that Lilly and Lucas had picked a table for two this time. Thank goodness for Oliver. Otherwise Miley would have nobody to hang with.

There were loads of things Miley and Oliver could have discussed. Like who last got booted off their favorite reality show or Oliver's recent discovery that their gym teacher had posted his profile on a popular online dating site. Or how Miley's dad was booking a summer concert tour for Hannah Montana and how it was going to be huge. But instead, they sat mesmerized, watching Lilly and Lucas share a raspberry smoothie. Every time they took a sip together, the tips of their noses touched. "Wow, would you look at that," Miley marveled.

"I know," Oliver said, scrunching up his nose in disgust. He glanced at the half-eaten burger next to Lilly. "Lilly's the queen of backwash. I bet he's sucking up bits of her burger right now."

Huh? Way for Oliver to miss the point completely! "This is a big moment for Lilly," Miley said with a sigh. "And if you had a romantic bone in your body, you'd be able to see that."

"Hey, I have eyes," Oliver argued. To prove it, he gave Miley the play-by-play of Lilly's date. "Look, he just said something funny, she laughed, big whoop."

"She's not laughing 'cause he's funny," Miley explained, rolling her eyes at Oliver's dim-wittedness. "She's laughing 'cause he's cute. Uch, boy brains. You might as well just scoop them out and store nuts up there." The whole Matt-Lilly-and-Miley-go-to-*Teen Court* episode should have taught Miley not to make sweeping generalizations about guys and girls. Except sometimes she forgot.

"Ohhh," said Oliver, puffing out his chest. "So girls laugh at me because I'm cute?"

Miley sighed. "No," she said, "girls laugh at *you* 'cause you nod like a chicken and fall over things."

"I do not!" he exclaimed. He spotted a girl walking by. This is the perfect opportunity to show Miley my smooth moves, he thought. "Hey, what up baby?" he called, leaning toward her and the group of girls with her while still seated in his chair. He suddenly lost his balance and toppled over. The girls laughed. Oops. Well, maybe Miley had a point after all.

"Oh, my gosh, I don't believe it!" Miley exclaimed, her eyes still peeled on Lilly and Lucas. "He just asked her to be his girlfriend!"

"How can you tell?" Oliver asked. As far

as he could tell, Lilly and Lucas were talking about video games. Or brussels sprouts. Or whether Crocs would still be in next year. (Oliver really hoped not.)

"Wait for it," Miley said knowingly. She leaned back and watched.

Within seconds they heard a gleeful screech, and then saw Lilly do a bold roundoff that led to a series of buoyant back handsprings. When something really good happened to Lilly, she broke out the gymnastics. She nailed her final back-tuck and found herself next to Oliver and Miley's table.

"He just asked me to be his girlfriend!" Lilly giddily cried. "Eeeep!"

"Eeeep!" Miley cheered. It was nice to see how happy having a boyfriend made Lilly. Miley gave her a congratulatory hug and then Lilly back-flipped away.

Chapter Two

Who knew so much could change in such a short amount of time? But in the nine days since becoming Lucas's girlfriend, Lilly had gone from smart and sassy to obsessive and sappy. She was all about Lucas, and Lucas was all about her.

What Miley wanted to know was: where did she, the best friend, fit in?

It was lunchtime, and Lilly and Lucas were having one of their typically boring conversations. Miley sat at the table in silence.

"You are so cute," swooned Lucas.

"You're cuter," Lilly cooed back.

"No, you're cuter."

"No, *you're* cuter."

Miley wasn't sure what was making her queasier: the cafeteria's bland french fries or Lilly and Lucas's inane conversation. "Yeah, you're both adorable," she quipped. "Can you pass the salt?"

There was no response. *Hel-lo,* was she invisible?

"I made you a mixed CD to celebrate the nine days we've spent together," Lucas told Lilly.

"It's right there, next to the pepper," Miley told them. She pointed to the salt-shaker.

Lilly anxiously grabbed the CD Lucas

had made for her. "Ohhhh," she cried, "the sound track of our love."

Meanwhile, Miley was still waiting for the salt. "Help me out, people," she snarled, aggravation rising. "I'm chewing on cardboard here."

"You make me so happy, Lilly-pad," Lucas said, a dreamy smile on his face.

Lilly-pad?! Ew!

"Not as happy as you make me, *Lukie-wookie*," Lilly responded.

Lukie-wookie! Ew, ew!

Suddenly Miley wasn't hungry anymore. "I think I'm going to pukie-wookie," she grumbled. It wasn't a very nice thing to say, but no one was listening to her anyway.

By the afternoon, Lilly had gone from bad to worse. Actually, Miley thought, make that worse to waaay worse. Miley didn't even know why Lilly was bothering to come over to Miley's house after school. She'd spent the entire walk from school gabbing on her cell phone to Lucas. "I don't want to say good-bye," Lilly said, tightly gripping her phone. "You hang up first." But apparently, Lucas couldn't bear to hang up either. They argued back and forth. "No, you," Lilly giggled.

"No, you," Lucas said.

Miley had had just about enough. She grabbed her cell phone out of her bag and speed-dialed Lilly.

"I'm getting another call," Lilly groaned. She put Lucas on hold. "Hello?" She didn't bother to hide her irritation at being interrupted.

"Hang up already!" Miley yelled as they both walked into the Stewarts' living room.

"Okay," Lilly huffed. What was Miley's

problem? She returned to the phone. "I gotta go," she told Lucas. And then it started all over again. "No, you," Lilly said coyly.

"No, you . . ."

"No, me!" Miley seethed. She grabbed Lilly's phone and flipped it shut. Phew!

"Hey!" Lilly looked mystified. "That was rude."

"You wanna talk rude?" Miley was too annoyed to hold back her anger. "This is the first time we've walked home together in nine days, and you spent the whole time going"—Miley held a pretend cell phone to her face—"'do you see that cloud, too? Let's make that our cloud. I love our cloud. Ow, I just ran into a tree. Oh, you ran into a tree, too? Aww!'" Her imitation of Lilly's voice was actually pretty good.

"I can't help it," Lilly confessed. "I just like him so much."

"I know," Miley said, softening. Despite her annoyance, she really did understand. She hadn't forgotten how crazy she'd been over Jake Ryan. "And I'm happy for you. I am. But I never see you anymore." It felt good to say the truth.

"Well, you could've sat with us at lunch today," Lilly snapped.

"I did!" Miley told her. *Whoa*. She knew they were oblivious to her, but not *that* oblivious.

"Really?" Lilly didn't remember Miley at the table at all. "Are you sure?"

"My point exactly!" Miley exclaimed. She stomped over to the couch and flopped down.

Lilly followed her. "I'm sorry," she said, sitting down next to Miley. "Hey, how about I come over Saturday and we do a movie night, just like we used to?"

"You're just doing that 'cause you feel sorry for me," Miley pouted. She wasn't going to be Lilly's charity case! But then she thought about how fun it'd be to hang out in pajamas and pig out on junk food all night. "But I'll take it," she said, brightening.

Just then, Lilly's phone rang. "Oh, go ahead," Miley told her, even though she had a feeling it was Lucas calling. The prospect of a fun girls' night had her feeling more forgiving.

Lilly quickly picked up the phone. "Hi," she said, smiling coyly. "Really?" She skipped over to the window and looked out. "Oh, you're right!" she exclaimed. "Our cloud is floating away! Bye, cloud! I'll miss you!"

Miley buried her face in a throw pillow and screamed. It was a dramatic gesture, but who cared? There was still no one paying attention to her.

Chapter Three

Miley's older brother, Jackson, never knew what to expect when he arrived for work at Rico's Surf Shop. One reason was that the boss he usually answered to wasn't Rico the dad, it was Rico the son. And Rico the son was just a kid. And while he was a very smart kid and also a very resourceful kid, he was still just a kid. When Jackson showed up for his after-school shift, he found Rico in a state of hysteria, alternately pounding his fists in despair and screaming up at the sky: "Why?! Why?! Why?! What did I do?!"

"Rico, what happened?" Jackson asked.

Rico took Jackson's hand and delicately broke the bad news to him: "We were robbed," he said, his upper lip quivering.

"You're kidding!" Jackson was stunned. The Surf Shop? Robbed? Who would do that? "How bad were we hit?"

Rico pointed ominously to the display rack of sunglasses. There was an empty hook where one pair was missing. "Look," said Rico. "Third one down! Just below the red ones! They're gone!"

One pair of sunglasses? Jackson should have known Rico was being dramatic. "A pair of sunglasses? This is *tragic*." He couldn't help himself from teasing Rico.

"Jackson, this is serious," Rico said crossly. "You don't get it. It's not just the sunglasses; they've stolen Rico's honor! And this will not stand." He thumped his chest defiantly.

Rico's honor? Rico had *honor*?

The next day was Saturday. On weekends, Jackson worked the morning shift. He was rarely fully awake when he got to the Surf Shop, so he counted on having a quiet hour before the store opened.

So when he reached the shop, he was surprised to see that Rico was already there. "Rico, what are you doing here so early?" Jackson asked sleepily.

"Just making sure my new security system works," Rico replied.

"What new security system?" Jackson

asked, hopping over the counter.

No sooner did Jackson's feet hit the floor then sirens began to blare.

"Riicccooooooo!!!" he screamed.

"*That* new security system," Rico said with a smirk.

Rico cupped his hands in imitation of a megaphone and roared, "Let this be a warning to all who dare challenge the power of the mighty Rico!"

A few hours later, Jackson had discovered that Rico's new top-notch security system was good for one thing only: making Jackson's life miserable. Actually, that wasn't true. It was good for something else: making customers lives' miserable, too.

Oliver leaned over the counter. "Hey, Jackson. Can I get a hot dog?"

"I dunno," Jackson said with a grimace. "How long do you have?"

Oliver was confused. "What do you mean?"

Jackson pressed a button on the hot-dog rotisserie display.

A robotic female voice instructed: "Please enter employee identification code."

"Jackson Stewart," Jackson droned. "Employee number zero-zero-zero-zero-zero-zero-zero-zero-zero . . . one."

"Welcome," said the robot voice. "Please enter your hot-dog access code."

Jackson pulled a dictionary-sized tome from behind the counter. He scanned the massive index. He began to read aloud. "All right, we've got chips; churros; fruit, fresh; fruit, frozen; fruit, smoothie; gum, bubble; gum, sugarless; hamburgers; hoagies. Oh, here we are . . . hot dogs." He punched a long series of numbers into the keypad and then listened for the beeps.

"Finally," said Oliver, who was pretty hungry at this point.

"You'd think," Jackson grumbled.

There were more beeps, then the robot voice came back. "Invalid entry," she said. "Wiener denied."

It was the twentieth time this had happened today. He'd already lost a bunch of customers, and his shift was only half over. "Oh, dang flabbit! I'm sick of this," Jackson complained. He pried open the glass door to the hot dog machine. He slipped the hot dog into a bun and handed it to Oliver.

"Intruder alert," the robot warned. "Activate trapdoor."

Trapdoor? Jackson didn't know about a trapdoor! Suddenly, the floor underneath him opened and — *Whooosh!* — Jackson fell out of sight.

"Jackson?" Oliver peered over the hole in the floor. He couldn't see anything, though he could hear distant groans. "Are you okay?"

"Get-et-et-et Rico-ico-ico-ico and a doctor-or-or-or. . . ." Jackson's desperate pleas echoed in the darkness.

I need a raise, Jackson thought.

Chapter Four

Miley loved everything about movie night. She loved shopping for it: roaming the aisles of the supermarket in search of the perfect junk food; studying the bins of pick-a-mix candy; trying to achieve the perfect mix of gummy bears and chocolate. She loved picking the movies—she and Lilly would text back and forth for days trying to figure out what to get. Then she loved coming home, changing into her pajamas, and setting up the living room so it was as comfortable as possible. Pillows had to be arranged so that your neck didn't cramp, snacks had to be so conveniently placed that you never had to move. . . . Having a cozy night in sure took a lot of work!

Lilly was coming in half an hour. Miley made sure she had everything.

DVDs lined up and ready to play? Check.

Extra blankets? Check.

Heaping bowl of their favorite caramel corn? Check.

Four different kinds of chips? Check, check, check, check.

Dips? Check six times.

"So, you all excited about movie night?" Mr. Stewart asked. Miley hadn't noticed her dad come downstairs.

"Yeah," she answered. "And just to let

you know, Dad, you are more than welcome . . . to skoodle your boodle outta
here." She gave her dad a big grin.

Mr. Stewart didn't look offended. "You
don't have to worry about that darlin',
cause I'm gonna be out in the garage re-
arranging some tools and listening to my
police scanner. That's the way a man
spends Saturday night."

"You really miss race-car season, don't
you, Daddy?" Miley said.

"Yeah, this time of year all they've got on
TV are those stupid dance shows," Mr.
Stewart said with a snort.

Miley actually liked those "stupid dance
shows," but she wasn't about to argue with
her dad. She just wanted him out of there.
She could hear footsteps coming toward
the front door. Lilly!

Miley knew the second Lilly stepped

inside the house that something was wrong. First of all, she looked nervous. Second of all, she sounded nervous. "Hi, hi," Lilly said in this awkward, too-excited way. But the real tip-off that something was definitely not right? Lilly was really dressed up. She was wearing the cute red cardigan she saved for special occasions and the new pink shirt she'd gotten at the mall. *And* she was wearing not only mascara but eye shadow. Eye shadow?

"Hey, what's going on?" Miley asked. "You're not in your movie jammies."

"Oh, right," Lilly stammered. She sounded almost frightened. "About that—"

"I mean that's a cute outfit, but it looks like you're going out with—" Just as Miley uttered his name, he walked into the house. "Lucas!"

Miley didn't know what to feel first:

shocked, enraged, or totally betrayed. This was supposed to be a girls' night! What was Lilly thinking?

"Hey, Miley, thanks for the invite," Lucas said, strolling in. Invite? As if! Miley felt the rage surge through her. Lucas didn't seem to notice the effect his presence was having. "I brought caramel corn," he added gamely.

"Great," Miley said in her most sarcastic way. "'Cause I only had enough for"—she glared at Lilly—"two."

Lilly looked at Miley nervously. "Could I talk to you in the kitchen?" she asked Miley.

"Just the two of us?" Miley asked snidely. "Alone? Are you sure?"

"Oh, Miley, you're so funny," Lilly said, her tone high and forced. When they got into the kitchen, she spoke in her normal voice. "I'm sorry," she said. "But he called at the last minute, and I told him I couldn't talk to him, but then he said, 'But you are talking,' and then I laughed and then he laughed and then I laughed—"

Miley wasn't sympathetic. "And to think I missed out on this yuck-fest—emphasis on the 'yuck!' You could've called to warn me."

"I was afraid you'd yell," Lilly squirmed.

"I can't believe you could be this selfish." Miley spat out the words. "You're the worst best friend ever."

Just then, there was a knock at the door. Now what? Lilly had another date? "Who's that?" Miley asked, stomping toward the door.

"Special delivery from your worst best friend ever," Lilly called out. "Come on in, Derek."

Derek? This night was going from bad to worse!

"You set me up on a blind date?" Miley was beside herself. "That is the most—" She stopped herself when she saw an absolutely adorable guy walking through the door. He had blond hair and light blue eyes, and he even dressed well. Not all guys could pick good jeans! Maybe this night could be rescued after all! She turned back to Lilly and said, "That is the most wonderful thing you've ever done for me." She whirled back around and smiled at Derek.

"Well, hello there," she said, putting on the charm.

"Hi, I'm Lucas's cousin, Derek." He smiled.

They stood there, looking coyly at each other. And then it dawned on Miley: she was wearing her pajamas!

She made a mad dash upstairs.

* * *

Miley should have known it was too good to be true. Her date with Derek went downhill as soon as the title sequence for the first movie started to roll.

Okay, yeah, he was cute. But he was also a huge scaredy-cat.

They'd picked a horror film to watch first, one Miley and Lilly had been waiting to see for ages. "You sure this movie isn't too scary for you guys?" Lucas asked.

"Not when I have you to protect me," Lilly replied, nuzzling closer to him.

Meanwhile, Miley and Derek sat watching the movie. Actually, Miley sat. Derek rocked back and forth in terror. "It's just a movie, it's just a movie . . ." he consoled himself as he cradled his knees in his arms.

"One of the worst . . . dates of . . . my

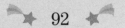

life . . ." Miley muttered so only Lilly could hear.

"I'm sorry," Lilly whispered back.

"Something's in there, something's in there!" Derek cried. He leaped toward the TV, knocking a bowl of popcorn out of Miley's hands. Just then, Mr. Stewart returned from organizing his tools in the garage—and it just so happened he had a chain saw in his hands. The sight of him sent Derek into a tizzy.

"I knew it!" Derek shricked, leaping into Miley's lap. He clutched at her, shivering in fear.

"Correction," Miley told Lilly. "*The* worst date of my life."

Chapter Five

That Monday, back at school, Miley told Oliver about her horrible date. "How could Lilly do that to me?" she moaned.

Oliver scratched his chin and raised his eyebrows thoughtfully. "You know she was just trying to hook you up so you didn't feel left out." His tone was sympathetic and understanding. "Sure it wasn't the one-on-one time you wanted, but it was still a very caring gesture."

For a second Miley wondered whether she was seeing and hearing things. Was this *Oliver* she was talking to? "Wow," she said, impressed. "Oliver, that was insightful, smart, and sensitive. What happened to your boy brain?"

"It spent last night checking out my mom's chick magazines," Oliver said with a shrug. "I learned that I'm an autumn, capri pants are best for my body shape, and new love is a bright flame that eventually dims to a warm, comfortable glow."

Miley slipped a couple of quarters into the vending machine. She considered Oliver's remarks. "Well, Lucas is her first real boyfriend," she said slowly.

"And she does seem to have achieved a new level of emotional satisfaction," Oliver replied.

Emotional satisfaction? Miley thought

that maybe Oliver read one too many magazines the night before.

"Okay, now you're seriously weirding me out," she said.

"Just go talk to her at lunch," Oliver suggested. "Oh, and the velvet belt . . . so last season." The bell rang, and Oliver headed to gym class.

Miley looked down at her belt. It *was* a year old. Maybe she shouldn't wear it anymore. Maybe those magazines *had* taught Oliver something she didn't know.

Miley headed to biology. As she walked toward the lab room, she chomped on her apple, wondering if both her best friends had changed forever. At least Oliver had become *more* sensitive—as opposed to Lilly!

Speaking of Lilly, there she was in the hallway with Lucas. Miley kept her head down and rushed past them. She had seen enough of Lilly and Lucas acting cutesy on Saturday night. Except something made her slow down.

Because the girl standing next to Lucas was not Lilly. And they were *kissing*.

Miley doubled back to get another look. Her eyes widened and she dropped her apple, shocked about what she had just witnessed.

Lucas was kissing another girl!

Chapter Six

Miley was in what her Uncle Earl would call "a pickle."

She had to tell Lilly her boyfriend was a smarmy, two-timing cheater. But after everything that had happened over the weekend, Miley didn't think Lilly would even believe her. Lilly thought Miley hated Lucas because she was jealous of the time he spent with Lilly. That might be true. Still, Lucas was a total sleaze!

Miley's head hurt just thinking about what she had to do. And the marching band practicing loudly in the cafeteria didn't make things better. Neither did the cafeteria's overhead fluorescent lights. She saw Lilly and Lucas sitting at a table. She got close enough so that she could hear what they were saying, but not so they could see her.

"She hasn't said a word to me all day," Miley heard Lilly moan. "She wouldn't even look at me in English. And when she looked at me in biology . . . daggers!"

Miley winced. She'd seen Lilly in biology right after witnessing the kiss. She hadn't known how to deal, so she'd avoided her.

"Hey, you've got a boyfriend who's crazy about you," Lucas explained. "It's gotta be tough for her." Miley watched Lucas slide his hand on top of Lilly's. Just seeing his sleazy paw on her made Miley's blood boil.

"You're so great," Lilly gushed. "I can't believe you're all mine."

"Well, believe it," Lucas said. "You're the only one for me." He leaned in closer to Lilly.

Miley had heard and seen enough! She swooped in just in time to interrupt the kiss. "Well, aren't you a busy boy?" she said to Lucas. Then she grabbed Lilly's shoulder. "Lilly, we need to talk." She guided her to a quieter spot in the cafeteria.

"Miley, I'm so sorry about the other night," Lilly said, once they were alone. "I was just—"

"Don't worry about it," Miley said quickly. "I need to tell you something: Lucas is cheating on you." The marching band picked just that moment to launch into their next number, so Lilly heard everything Miley said except the "cheating on you" part.

"What?" Lilly asked.

Miley raised her voice. "Lucas is cheating on you!"

Boy that trombone was loud!

"What?" Lilly asked again.

Miley screamed this time. "LUCAS IS CHEATING ON YOU." Suddenly Miley realized the music had stopped playing, and now a hush had fallen over the cafeteria. Everyone was looking at her, including Lucas.

"W-w-what?" Lilly reeled.

"It's true," Miley replied quietly. She hated that everyone had heard. Poor Lilly didn't need to be publicly humiliated. She whipped around to face Lucas. "Yeah, tell her, Lu-kiss-every-girl-in-school."

"Lilly, I feel horrible about this," Lucas said, running over to them.

"A little late in the day for that, bub,"

Miley snapped, putting her arm around Lilly protectively.

"I'm so sorry that your best friend is so threatened by our relationship she'd lie to break us up," Lucas continued.

Hey, wait a second, that didn't sound like a confession! Miley thought. She couldn't believe what she was hearing!

"So, it's not true?" Lilly asked Lucas.

"Of course not," Lucas lied.

"Come on, Lilly, who are you going to believe?" Miley countered. "That lip-lock liar or your best friend?"

Lilly looked from Miley to Lucas and back again. "C'mon, Lucas," she said finally. She led Lucas away, leaving Miley alone with the marching band.

Now what?

Miley was going to have to try something

else, that's what. She couldn't let Lilly keep going out with Lucas. She'd do whatever it took to make Lilly realize that Lucas was a two-timing jerk. And she had to do something quickly—and not only because she needed to free Lilly from Lucas's slimeball clutches. She missed Lilly. The sooner she showed her who the real Lucas was, the sooner she'd have her best friend back.

The plan was Oliver's idea. He'd read two articles in his mom's magazines about plotting revenge, so—according to him— he was basically an expert. All Miley had to do, Oliver claimed, was to get Lucas to fall for *her*. Then Oliver would hide somewhere and capture them on video. The only problem was: the only good place to hide was the garbage can.

Oliver settled in among the rotting tuna sandwiches and crumpled-up pieces of paper. Meanwhile, Miley waited for Lucas outside his locker. Finally, he swaggered over, still sipping his milk shake from lunch. "Hello there," she sang, batting her lashes provocatively.

"Miley." Lucas raised his eyebrows in surprise. "What are you doing here?"

"I just came to tell you that you were right," Miley said breathily. She knew how corny he was with Lilly, so she laid it on. "I was jealous. But not of you. Of her with you. I want to be with you. I want to find puffy little clouds with you."

"Miley—" Lucas said.

She interrupted him. "No, no, no," she said coyly. "Don't speak. Just kiss me." As soon as she spoke, she reconsidered her choice of words. Why leave it up to chance? "No, I'll kiss you," she said.

She braced herself for the horror of

Lucas's lips on hers. She was going to have to use some serious mouthwash after this. She leaned in, so that her face was centimeters away from his. Miley pursed her lips, tightly closed her eyes, and waited.

But nothing happened.

She waited some more.

Still nothing.

Miley opened her eyes, unpursed her lips, and looked at Lucas in confusion. He was sneering at her. "Nice try," he said slyly. "But I think you and I both know the kind of guy I really am." Miley watched as he strutted off, tossing the remains of his milk shake into the garbage can and onto poor Oliver's head.

"What was I thinking?" Miley growled at the garbage can. Oliver stuck his head out. He was covered in bits of trash. "He's never going to hit on Lilly's best friend. I had to try something. I mean it's not like I can just put on some disguise and . . ."

Suddenly something clicked in her head. A disguise? Of course! As Hannah Montana, Miley spent almost half her life in disguise. Why hadn't she thought of that? She could totally woo Lucas as Hannah! "Boy, am I stupid!" Miley said as Oliver shook the remains of Lucas's milk shake out of his hair.

Chapter Seven

Another weekend at Rico's, and the new security system was still driving Jackson crazy.

Today he was really in a rush. He was late for a date with Lisa, a girl he'd just met, but he still had to close up the shop. And with the new alarm features, that was a very complicated process. He had to make sure every machine was individually locked—the hot-dog machine, the milk-shake maker, the deep fryer. Then he had to enable the trapdoor and the infrared detection devices.

After doing all that, Jackson was so frantic that he forgot his keys. "Keys!" he said, then jumped over the counter to get them.

He was in midair when he realized what he'd done. The alarms! "Intruder alert. Intruder alert," warned the robot voice. "Activate deep freeze."

By the time Rico arrived, Jackson was standing perfectly still, his entire body encrusted with ice. He'd missed his date with Lisa, he'd lost all the feeling in his feet and hands, and his tongue was stuck to the roof of his mouth. Even his brain felt frozen. The only thing he could think to say when he saw Rico was: "That's it,

R-R-R-R-ico." His teeth were chattering so badly, he could barely form the words. "I q-q-q-q-quit."

Jackson might be a pain, but he was a loyal worker. Rico's dad wouldn't like it if Jackson quit. So, Rico did his best to improve the situation. He gave Jackson towels and blankets and even some free hot dogs. Jackson's lips were quivering too much to eat them, but he pressed them against his skin for warmth.

Finally, when he'd warmed up enough, he turned to Rico and asked: "Why are you doing this? I mean, you spent a fortune on a security system because of a seven-dollar pair of sunglasses. And all it's done is kill your business and freezer-burn my butt! It doesn't make sense."

"It does to me," Rico explained. "I don't want anyone thinking they can take advantage of me because of my size. I don't care how much it costs, no human being will ever rip off Rico again." Jackson didn't know how to respond to Rico's proclamation. After everything, he couldn't help feeling sorry for the little guy.

Their silence was suddenly interrupted by a rustling sound. And it was coming from inside the shop! First there was scratching, then scraping. Jackson turned to look. It was the thief! He had piercing black eyes and sharp teeth, and he brazenly sported the stolen sunglasses around his neck. He also had gray fur and really sharp claws.

The thief was a raccoon.

Jackson and Rico watched as the animal sunk its sharp teeth into a hot dog. "I hope he enjoys it," Rico said mournfully, looking at all his new equipment. "That hot dog cost me eleven thousand dollars."

Chapter Eight

Usually, when Miley dressed up as Hannah Montana, it was because she was performing onstage or making a special appearance. When she actually had down time, she wanted to spend it just hanging out as herself. As Miley.

But every now and then, she had to admit, it was fun to dress up as Hannah and go out on the town. She knew it was unfair that celebrities got treated better than everyone else. But sometimes the perks were irresistible!

For instance, the restaurant she'd picked for what she and Oliver had nicknamed "The Lucas Intervention" was the hottest place in Southern California. Most people had to wait months to get a reservation. All Miley had to do was call from her cell phone two minutes before she got there. It helped that she was on a first-name basis with the maître d'.

She and Lilly had to fight their way through the throngs of people waiting to be seated. "Wow," said Lilly as they made their way to the front of the line. "When you apologize, you don't fool around. This is the coolest restaurant in town." Lilly was dressed as Hannah Montana's right-hand girl, Lola Luftnagle. She wore a hot pink wig, a black-and-white checkered miniskirt, and a strand of black beads around her neck.

"Well it's the least I could do after the way I acted," Miley said humbly. She and Oliver had decided that their best strategy was for Miley to pretend she'd been wrong about Lucas. Then they'd let Lilly discover the truth for herself.

"Hannah!" the maître d' cried.

"Phillipe!" Miley exclaimed. "I'm so sorry I called at the last minute!"

"Don't give it a second thought," Phillipe said, ushering her inside. He called out to his waiters: "Table for Miss Montana!" A team of waiters suddenly entered the room, carrying a table for two over their heads. Apparently, when Hannah Montana calls and you don't have a table for her, you *get* one.

Miley let Lilly walk ahead of her, so she

wouldn't see her scanning the dining area for Oliver and Lucas. Oliver's mom had a friend who was a pastry chef at the restaurant, so he'd been able to score a reservation also. The plan was for Oliver to bring Lucas, and then for Miley to flirt with him. Only this time it would be Hannah Montana doing the flirting!

Miley and Lilly's table had a clear view of where Lucas and Oliver were sitting. She was going to have to do her flirting without Lilly catching on, and *that* was going to be a challenge. "I'm just so glad we're not fighting anymore," Lilly said happily, taking a sip of water. "And, you know, once you get to know Lucas, I know you guys are going to be really close friends."

Lilly lifted up her menu and started to look it over. Miley glanced over at the boys' table and made eye contact with Lucas.

She gave him a wink and a wave, and then watched as he gasped in surprise. Then he turned to Oliver, practically panting, and exclaimed: "Dude, that's Hannah Montana! And she's totally checkin' me out!"

"You're kidding!" Oliver replied incredulously, playing along. "Where?" Lucas motioned to Miley and Lilly's table. Miley blew him a kiss. Lucas practically fell out of his chair.

Miley smiled. Their plan was working!

After they'd ordered their appetizers, Miley excused herself to use the ladies' room, making a point of passing Oliver and Lucas's table on her return. "Oh, I am so sorry," she said, purposely stumbling so that her fingers grazed the back of Lucas's head. "Great hair," she whispered.

She hadn't moved even two steps away

when she heard Lucas brag, "Did you see that? That was a move."

"Not just *a* move," Oliver told him. "That was a hair-touch move."

"You're right," Lucas said. "She wants me." He paused, then sounded tentative. "It's too bad I'm going with Lilly."

It was the moment Oliver had been waiting for, and he pounced. "I have two words for you: 'guy code.' We are men. We are hunters. And what happens in the jungle, it stays in the jungle."

Miley had to stop herself from laughing out loud and blowing her cover. It was funny to hear Oliver sound so boy-brained, when just yesterday he was telling her that hot lemon juice mixed with verbena oil was the key to a clear complexion.

"Dude, you rock!" Lucas exclaimed. "And if things work out, I'll hook you up with her friend." He pointed to Hannah Montana's magenta-headed friend, none other than Lilly.

"Fingers crossed," Miley heard Oliver say. Satisfied, she returned to her table.

"Look," said Lilly, her mouth full of shrimp cocktail. Their appetizers had arrived, and she couldn't wait to start. She pointed across the room. "Justin Timberlake is eating the same shrimp as me. Hey, Justin. Great shrimp, huh?" With Lilly's attention on the celebrity two tables over, Miley gave Lucas another little wave. He waved back.

"What are you doing?" Lilly asked.

"Nothing," Miley said quickly, returning to her shrimp. Shoot! She'd have to be more careful!

But it was too late. Lilly knew Miley was up to something. "You got your flirting face on," she accused. "Who is he?" She swiveled around to get a view of the crowd. "Is it that guy?" she asked. "Or that guy?" Miley prayed that somehow she'd miss Lucas and Oliver's table. "Or that guy?" Lilly asked. "Or Lucas, or Oliver? Or . . ."

Lucas and Oliver?

It didn't take long for Lilly to figure out what was going on. "Ohhhh, you're despicable," she growled.

"Lilly, I had to do something to show you I wasn't lying," she pleaded.

"The only thing you've shown me is that we're no longer friends!" Lilly yelled angrily, standing up. "I am leaving."

"I'm just trying to protect you from getting hurt!" Miley insisted. How could she convince her?

"The only one who's hurting me is you," Lilly argued. "You just can't accept the fact that Lucas really cares about me."

Just then Miley saw Lucas rise from his table and give his hair one last tousle. Finally! He was making his move! "Oh yeah?" she asked Lilly. "Then why is he coming over here to flirt with Hannah?"

Lilly sat back down. She was as desperate as Miley to prove she was right. "He's coming over here to tell you to stop making googly eyes at him because he has a girlfriend," she said stubbornly.

A moment later, Lucas was grinning at them. "Hi, Hannah, I'm Lucas. I noticed you looking at me and, uh . . ."

Miley wanted to get this over with. "Go ahead, just say it," she coaxed him.

"Yeah, tell her how you really feel," Lilly grumbled.

"Well . . . the truth is . . ." It was the moment Miley had been waiting for, and just her luck, it was interrupted. A woman dragging an eight-year-old girl pushed her way past Lucas. "Excuse me, Miss Fontana," the woman said. "I have your biggest fan right here."

The girl blushed. "Grandma." She groaned in embarrassment.

As much as Miley wanted to tell them she was busy, she couldn't. Hannah Montana had responsibilities to her fans. "Don't go anywhere," Miley told Lucas. "This will just take a second." She grabbed a piece of paper and signed her name. "There you go, sweetie," she told the girl.

Now, back to Lucas. Except now the woman wanted a picture, too. "It'll just take a second," she told Miley. "All right, now, smile." Miley and the girl posed.

The woman fiddled with the settings on her camera while Miley waited, her face frozen in a wide smile. She tapped her foot impatiently. "Oh, not here," the woman said finally. "The lighting isn't good here. It's better in the bathroom. Let's go."

Miley was about to make an excuse, but the woman grabbed her elbow and started pulling, while the granddaughter begged her to stop. "Just tell *her* what you were going to say," Miley instructed Lucas.

"Yeah. Uh, what was it you were going to say?" Lilly asked.

Lucas handed Lilly the folded-up piece of paper. "Can you just give Hannah Montana my number?" he asked. "And tell her to call anytime."

Miley was halfway to the bathroom, so she couldn't see that Lilly's face had fallen. But she heard the desperation in her voice. "W-w-w-why?" Lilly asked. "To tell her you have a girlfriend? 'Cause, you know, you look like the kind of guy who has a girlfriend he really really likes."

"Actually," Lucas commented arrogantly, "I've got two."

"Two?" Lilly's voice cracked.

"Yep," he said with a smirk. "But I'd dump 'em both for Hannah."

When Miley returned from the bathroom, Lucas was covered in shrimp cocktail. His cheeks were smeared with sticky red sauce, and a shrimp was stuck in the collar of his shirt.

"Oooh, you really got that boy back good," Miley said, sitting down.

"That was just Lola," Lilly scowled. "Wait till *Lilly* gets hold of him."

Miley was happy to hear the toughness in Lilly's voice. Still, she felt bad that Lucas had lied to Lilly. "Lilly, I'm really sorry," she said sincerely.

"Yeah, I'm really sorry I didn't believe

you," Lilly replied. "Wow, boys can really mess things up, can't they?"

Didn't Miley know it!

"So, what are we going do next time one of us has a boyfriend?" Lilly asked.

"The only thing we can do," Miley answered. "Trust each other. Deal?"

"Deal," said Lilly. They raised their water glasses, then clinked.

By the time their main courses arrived, Lucas was gone, and Miley and Lilly's friendship was back on track. They ordered extra fries, then two desserts. Then they went back to Miley's house, got into their coziest jammies, filled bowls with chips and caramel popcorn, settled into the couch, and watched horror movies.

Miley smiled to herself as she grabbed a handful of popcorn. Just like old times, she thought happily.

Put your hands together for the next Hannah Montana book . . .

Wishful Thinking

Adapted by Laurie McElroy

Based on the series created by Michael Poryes and Rich Correll & Barry O'Brien

Based on the episode, "When You Wish You Were The Star," Written by Douglas Lieblein

Hannah Montana's strong, clear voice filled the arena. She was bringing another amazing concert to a close. The audience cheered loudly as she sang the last note of the song. She waved good-bye to her fans before dashing backstage and into her dressing room.

"Hannah, you rock! I can't believe you did three encores!" Lola Luftnagle said loudly. She closed the dressing-room door to make sure they were alone, and then said, "I can't believe you did three encores. You know we have a science project due Monday. What is wrong with you?"

Hannah Montana wasn't just a teen superstar, she was also a regular high school girl named Miley Stewart. And Lola Luftnagle was really Lilly Truscott, Miley's best friend.

"Oh. Oh, okay," Miley said. "Let's leave this boring rock-star life behind and get back to the glamorous world of earthworm larvae."

At that moment, Hannah Montana's bodyguard, Roxy, poked her head into the dressing room. "You decent, girl?" she asked.

Just then, Jesse McCartney walked into the room. "Hi, I'm Jesse," he said.

"Oh, my gosh," Miley babbled, bouncing up and down. "It's Jesse McCartney! I'm a big fan. *Big* fan!"

Jesse smiled. "Listen, tonight *I'm* the fan. You did a great job. Listen, Hannah, a bunch of my friends and I are going to the Dragon Room tonight. You want to come?"

"Yes!" Miley squealed.

"No!" Lilly said at the same time. "Our science project," Lilly whispered.

"Oh, right," Miley said. But there was no way she could admit she had homework without telling Jesse about her double life. He knew her only as Hannah Montana. Pop stars didn't have school commitments. Miley couldn't explain without revealing her secret.